ALICE in WONDERLAND

Curiouser and Curiouser

Published by Creative Edge, LLC, 2010, an imprint of Dalmatian Press, LLC, Franklin, Tennessee 37067.
No part of this book may be reproduced or copied in any form without written permission from the copyright owner.

Printed in China

10 11 ZHE 10 9 8 7 6 5 4 3 2 1
CE12819

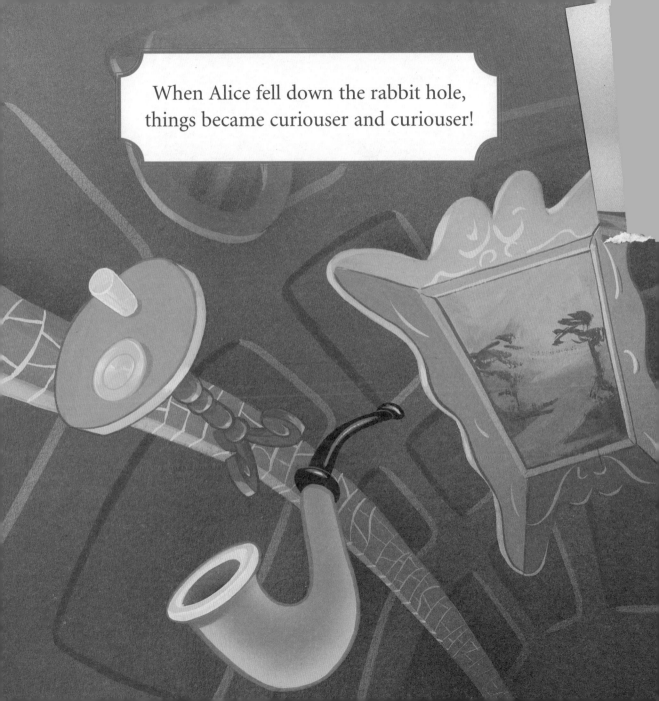

When Alice fell down the rabbit hole,
things became curiouser and curiouser!

Most peculiar!
Odd creatures in a pool of tears!

Just a bit silly!
A Walrus and Carpenter coaxing oysters.

How absurd!
Alice sprouts up in a house!

*Very extraordinary!
A garden of talking flowers!*

Strange, indeed!
Tea for three—served up with foolishness.

So bizarre!
A brooming, brushy dog.
Why, thank you!

Quite unusual!
A Cat atop a Queen at croquet!

Oh, wonderful!
A door with a talking Doorknob!
Will it take Alice home?

Or was it all just a wonder-filled dream?